The Tale of Thomas Mead

Alphabet

by Pat Hutchins

Greenwillow
Read-alone

GREENWILLOW BOOKS
New York

First Edition   1 2 3 4 5 6 7 8 9 10

Library of Congress Cataloging in Publication Data
Hutchins, Pat (date)   The tale of Thomas Mead.
(Greenwillow read-alone books)
Summary: Thomas refuses to learn to read and gets
into trouble when he fails to read signs like "Exit,"
"Danger," and "Ladies."   [1.   Reading—Fiction]
I.   Title.   PZ7.H96165Tal   [E]   79-6398
ISBN 0-688-80282-6   ISBN 0-688-84282-8 lib. bdg.

To the Children of the

Des Plaines, Illinois

Public Library

There was a boy called Thomas Mead
who never ever learned to read.
"I wish you would!" his teacher sighed.
"Why should I?" Thomas Mead replied.

Well, one day Thomas went out walking.
He heard the men above him talking,
but couldn't read the sign that said,
"DANGER—workmen overhead."

A pot of paint fell through the air,
and changed the color of his hair.
"Can't you read?" the workmen cried.
"Why should I?" Thomas Mead replied.

A lady said, "What a disgrace!
Why don't you clean your hair and face?"
She pointed to a big glass door.
"There's a bathroom in that store."

He pushed the PULL sign on the door,
and knocked some shoppers to the floor.
"Can't you read?" the shoppers cried.
"Why should I?" Thomas Mead replied.

A friendly sales clerk told him where
he could clean his face and hair.
"The bathroom's on the seventh floor,
the elevator's by the door."

Then she murmured with a frown,

"You should have pressed the UP, not DOWN!"

"Can't you read?" a small boy cried.

"Why should I?" Thomas Mead replied.

The friendly sales clerk shook her head.
"I'd better take you there," she said.
She took him up the seven floors,
and pointed to the washroom doors.

Thomas marched in . . .

but in vain—

a lady chased him out again.

"Can't you read?" the lady cried.

"Why should I?" Thomas Mead replied.

Quite a crowd had come to stare
at Thomas and his emerald hair.

So Thomas thought he'd leave the store,
and ran downstairs toward a door.

A wagon, laden to the brim,

tipped its load all over him.

"Can't you read?" the storeman cried.

"Why should I?" Thomas Mead replied.

Thomas, looking less than neat,
left the store to cross the street.

He walked up to the yellow lines,

but couldn't read the "DON'T WALK" signs.

With screaming brakes cars rammed each other,
a passing policeman sighed, "Oh, brother!"

"Can't you read?" The drivers cried.

"Why should I?" Thomas Mead replied.

"I'll tell you why!" the policeman said,
and from a little notebook read,
"'Jaywalking.' That's a serious crime.
You'll have to pay an instant fine!"

And as poor Thomas couldn't pay,
a police car carried him away.

They locked him up and called his ma,
who came to see him with his pa.

Ma and Pa had both agreed,

that Thomas really ought to read.

"Bail me out, Pa!" Thomas cried.

"When you can read!" his ma replied.

His cellmates thought it was a crime
that Thomas Mead was doing time,
and all because he couldn't read.
"Please help me to!" cried Thomas Mead.

They taught him words he ought to know,

like UP and DOWN, and STOP and GO,

IN and OUT, EMPTY, FULL,

EXIT, ENTRANCE, PUSH and PULL,

and BATHROOM, LADIES, GENTLEMEN,

and DANGER, WET PAINT, WALK, DON'T RUN,

and then they said they'd better get,

him started on the alphabet.

The policeman was surprised to see
how soon Tom learned his ABC.
"Well done!" he shouted. "You can read!"
"Of course I can!" said Thomas Mead.

Now Thomas, who is reading well,
has long since left his prison cell.

He reads all day, and then at night
he switches on his bedside light

and reads until his parents say,

"Thomas! Put that book away!"

"I wish you would!" his mother sighs.

But Thomas sleepily replies,
"Why should I?"

PAT HUTCHINS was awarded England's prestigious Kate Greenaway Medal for *The Wind Blew,* the best picture book of 1974. Since the publication of her first picture book, *Rosie's Walk,* in 1968, reviewers on both sides of the Atlantic have been loud in their praises.

Among her popular books are *One-Eyed Jake; Happy Birthday, Sam; Don't Forget the Bacon!; The Best Train Set Ever,* and two novels for young readers—*The House That Sailed Away* and *Follow That Bus!* Pat Hutchins, her husband Laurence, and their two sons, Morgan and Sam, live in London, England.